SUPER-PETS!

By Billy Wrecks • Illustrated by Ethen Beavers

A GOLDEN BOOK • NEW YORK

Copyright © 2016 DC Comics.
DC SUPER FRIENDS and all related characters and elements
are trademarks of and © DC Comics.
WB SHIELD: ™ & © Warner Bros. Entertainment Inc.
(s16)

DC COMICS™

RHUS35331

randomhousekids.com   ISBN 978-0-553-53923-3 (trade) — ISBN 978-0-553-53924-0 (ebook)

Printed in the United States of America   10 9 8 7 6 5 4 3 2 1

Batman, Superman, and Wonder Woman were the guests of honor at the **Metropolis Pet Show**. People from all over the city came to show off their pets—and maybe win the big $10,000 prize!

"We are delighted to have the Super Friends with us today," the judge told the roaring crowd. "And their amazing Super-Pets!"

Streaky the Super-Cat
flew through the air . . .

Wonder Woman's
kangaroo, **Jumpa**,
bounced and jumped . . .

. . . and **Ace** the **Bat-Hound** looked around, sniffing the air. He was always ready for trouble—just like Batman.

"Now let's see all these wonderful pets," the judge declared. The people and animals lined up. They began to parade past the judge and the Super Friends.

Ace sniffed again, and growled. Something smelled suspicious. The Dog Detective barked—

"The Joker!" Batman exclaimed as Ace pointed at one of the pet owners. "With his hyenas, **Crackers** and **Giggles**!"

"And Cheetah, with **Chauncey** the cat!" Wonder Woman said, spotting the feline villainess.

"Come out, Croc," Superman called.
"I see you—and **Anna Conda**, too."
"They must be here to steal the prize
money," Wonder Woman said.

"I promise we're not up to any funny business," the Joker said. "We just want our pets to be in the show!"

Giggles and Crackers howled in agreement.

"There's no rule against super-villains being in the show," the judge declared. "I suggest we have a contest of Super-Pets!" The crowd cheered.

Ace barked. Streaky meowed. Jumpa nodded.

"They'll do it!" said Wonder Woman.

"While we keep an eye on the bad guys," Batman added.

The judge said the first contest would be a high jump.

"Hop to it," Wonder Woman told Jumpa. To everyone's surprise, Anna Conda coiled herself into a spring and bounced higher than Jumpa!

The second contest was an obstacle course. Ace dashed through it in record time. But Crackers and Giggles didn't even finish—they crashed into each other at the starting line!

"That's okay, boys. We can still laugh about it," the Joker said.

The final contest was a race between Streaky and Chauncey. But as soon as the cats started, Streaky saw something. He couldn't believe his super-vision—the judge was stealing the prize money!

Ace barked, and all
the pets leapt into action!

Jumpa leaned back on her tail and used her powerful legs to launch Chauncey into the air.

Chauncey nimbly bounced off the lamppost and into the judge's chest. Ace and Crackers pulled Anna Conda tight like a rope, tripping the judge. He fell backward.

Giggles and Streaky made sure that the
judge couldn't get away. Ace pulled away
the judge's disguise, revealing—

"The Penguin!" Cheetah snarled in surprise. "Only a villain as **fowl** as you would try to steal money from the Pet Show."

Batman turned the Penguin over to the guards while Superman put the prize money back in its rightful place.

"Today has been *grrrreat*," Croc rumbled, hugging Anna Conda.

"Having the love of a good pet makes us all winners," Wonder Woman said. The crowd cheered in agreement.

And with that, Ace, Streaky,
Jumpa, and the Super Friends
raced off to their next adventure!